Alice's Adventures in Wonderland

A classic story by Lewis Carroll
Adapted by Gill Munton

Contents

CHAPTER 1

The White Rabbit

Alice was sitting next to the river with her sister, who was reading a book. It was a hot summer day and soon Alice started to feel very sleepy. She lay down and closed her eyes.

'Shall I pick some flowers?' Alice wondered …

Then she heard footsteps and a White Rabbit ran past! He had pink eyes, pink ears and a pink nose with long whiskers. He wore a jacket and a waistcoat and he carried a little umbrella. The White Rabbit took a gold watch from his waistcoat pocket and looked at it.

'I'm late! I'm late! Oh, what shall I do?' the White Rabbit cried, twitching his little pink nose. He started running again, even faster.

Alice watched him. 'That's very strange!' she thought. 'A rabbit, in a jacket and a waistcoat, with a gold watch in his pocket! I'll follow him and see where he goes.'

So Alice jumped up and ran after the White Rabbit. He went across a field. When he got to the end of the field, he jumped down into a rabbit hole. Alice jumped down after him.

Alice fell down, down the rabbit hole. The hole was very deep. Alice tried to look down, but it was too dark at the bottom. She did see lots of things around her as she fell. There were cupboards and bookshelves and pictures and maps and even a little jar. The label on the jar said 'JAM', but when Alice picked it up and looked inside, she saw that it was empty. Alice was disappointed.

'That's bad luck!' she thought. 'But what shall I do with the jar? I won't drop it down the rabbit hole. It might hit someone.' So she put it safely in one of the cupboards.

Down, down she fell.

'When will I get to the bottom?' she wondered. 'At home, I cry if I fall down the stairs. But I won't cry next time – this is much worse! Mother and Father will think I'm very brave. Perhaps I'll fall to the centre of the earth! I think that's about four thousand miles …'

(Alice was a clever little girl and she had learnt this in one of her geography lessons.)

'Or perhaps I'll fall to the other side of the earth – to Australia! Do people in Australia walk upside down?' Alice wondered.

Down, down, down.

Alice felt lonely and she started to think about her pet cat, Dinah. 'Dinah will be sad tonight if I am not at home with her. I hope Mother will remember to give her a bowl of milk. Oh, my dear Dinah! Why aren't you in the rabbit hole with me? There are no mice for you to catch here because mice can't fly, but perhaps there are some bats. A bat is just a mouse with wings. Do cats catch bats, Dinah?'

Alice was very sleepy now. 'Do cats catch bats? Do bats catch cats? I don't know,' she said, her eyes closing.

Then suddenly: Thump! Alice reached the bottom of the rabbit hole. She was lying on a pile of sticks and dry leaves. The long fall was over.

Alice jumped up and looked around her. She saw a long tunnel and the White Rabbit was running along it.

'I'm late! I'm late! Oh, my ears and whiskers!' the White Rabbit cried. He twitched his pink nose and ran round a corner.

'I must be quick,' thought Alice. 'I want to know where he's going.'

Alice followed him, but he had disappeared.

Alice was now in a long, low room. Some lamps hung from the ceiling and there were lots of doors. Alice tried to open each door, but they were all locked. 'How will I get out?' she sighed. 'I can't stay here forever!'

She saw a little glass table with only three legs. A tiny gold key lay on top of it and Alice picked it up. She tried t

4

unlock each door, but the key didn't fit any door. It was too small. Then she noticed a green curtain and looked behind it.

There was a tiny door behind the curtain – and the key fitted the lock! She opened the door and looked in.

Alice saw a beautiful garden. The sun was shining brightly, and there were lots of pink and white flowers and fruit trees and cool water fountains.

'I must go into that garden,' Alice thought. 'I want to walk among the trees and smell the flowers. But I'm much too big – I can't fit through the tiny door. Oh, what shall I do?'

Alice went back to the little table and put the gold key on it. 'Perhaps I'll find another key,' she thought.

She did not find a key – but she found a little bottle. 'That bottle wasn't here before,' said Alice. 'What's in it?'

She picked the bottle up. A label was tied round it. The label said 'DRINK ME'. Alice thought for a minute.

'Perhaps it's poison,' she said. 'If I drink poison, I'll die! I'll check.' (Alice was a sensible child.)

She looked carefully at the bottle, but she did not see the word 'POISON'. 'I think I'll try it,' she thought. And she did.

'Mmmm. It's very nice,' Alice thought. 'I can taste oranges and apples and roast chicken!' She drank some more and soon the bottle was empty.

'I feel very strange,' Alice said to herself. 'I think I'm shrinking.'

And she was! She got smaller and smaller, and soon she was the same size as the little door behind the green curtain.

Alice was very pleased. 'I can go into the garden now,' she thought. 'But I'll wait for a minute. Perhaps I'll shrink more. Perhaps I'll disappear – like the flame of a candle!'

A few minutes later, Alice thought, 'I don't think I'll shrink any more. I'll go into the garden now.'

So she went back to the little door – but it was locked again and she did not have the key! 'Now what shall I do?' she cried. 'The key is on the table – but I can't reach it! I'm too small now!'

She tried to climb up one of the table legs, but she could not get to the top. It was too high. Poor Alice sat down and started to cry. 'Stop crying, you silly child,' she told herself. 'Crying won't help.'

Then she saw something under the table. 'It's a little glass box!' she cried.

She picked up the box and opened it. Alice found a tiny cake inside the box. On the top of the cake, the words 'EAT ME' were spelt out in raisins.

'I'll eat some of it,' thought Alice. 'If it makes me bigger, I can reach the key. If it makes me smaller, I can crawl under the door!' So she started to eat the cake.

She waited for a minute. Nothing happened. She didn't get bigger and she didn't get smaller.

'I'll eat it all,' thought Alice. And she did.

CHAPTER 2

The pool of tears

'Goodbye, feet!' said Alice, looking down at them.

The cake had made her as tall as a tree and her feet were a long way from her head.

'Oh, my poor feet! Who will put on your shoes and socks every morning? I can't do it,' Alice said. 'I can't reach you. But I must be kind to you. I'll send you a new pair of boots every year.'

She started to laugh. 'How silly – sending presents to my feet!' she said. 'The address on the parcel will look very strange.'

> To
> Alice's Right Foot
> The Floor
> Near the Cupboard
> With Love from Alice

'Ouch! I've hit my head on the ceiling! I'm still growing! But I can get the key now,' thought Alice.

Alice picked up the tiny gold key from the table and went back to the little door. She opened it, but now she was too big to fit through it! So she put the key back on the glass table. Then she sat down and started to cry again.

'Stop that!' she told herself. 'You're too big to cry like that!'

But she did not stop. She cried and cried and cried. Because she was so big now, there was soon a huge pool of tears.

After a short time, she heard little footsteps and quickly dried her eyes. It was the White Rabbit again. This time he was dressed in a nice blue coat. He carried a pair of white gloves and a large fan.

'I'm late!' the White Rabbit cried. 'I'm late for the Duchess! She'll be so angry with me. Oh, my ears and whiskers!'

'Please, sir,' Alice asked the White Rabbit politely, 'will you help me?'

But when he saw Alice, the White Rabbit was afraid. He ran away into the darkness, dropping his gloves and his fan. Alice picked them up.

'This is such a strange day,' she sighed. 'Am I still Alice? I'm not my friend Ada because she has curly, dark hair and I have straight, blonde hair. I'm not Mabel because I'm clever and she is not. I know lots of things. I'll try to remember some of them.

'Four times five is twelve – oh, that's not right!' she said. 'Four times six is thirteen – oh no, I've forgotten how to

do maths! I'll try geography. London is the capital of Paris and Paris is the capital of Rome – no, that's wrong, too! I'll try to say a poem:

> *How does the little crocodile*
> *Improve his shining tail,*
> *And pour the waters of the Nile*
> *On every golden scale!*

How cheerfully he seems to grin,
How neatly spreads his claws,
And welcomes little fishes in,
With gently smiling jaws!

'I think those are the wrong words!' said Alice. 'That poem isn't about a crocodile – it's about a bee. Perhaps I really am Mabel!'

Alice looked down at her hands. They were getting smaller and smaller.

'Oh!' she cried. 'I've picked up the White Rabbit's fan and it's making me shrink again.' She dropped the fan quickly. 'Now I can go into the beautiful garden,' she said.

But when she went back to the little door, it was locked again. The key was on the table and she was too small to reach it. 'Now what shall I do?' she asked herself.

As she spoke, she slipped and fell into the pool of tears with a splash. The water came up to her chin and some of it went in her mouth. It tasted salty.

'Have I fallen into the sea?' Alice wondered. 'If I have, I can go home on the train.' (She had been to the sea once with her mother and father, and they had travelled by train.)

And then she thought, 'No, you silly child, it's not the sea. It's a huge pool of tears. Oh, why did I cry so much when I was big?'

Alice swam round and round the pool, trying to find a way out. Then she heard a big splash on the other side of the pool.

'I'll swim across the pool and find out what it is,' she decided. 'Perhaps it's a turtle or even an octopus. But that can't be right. I'm tiny now, so perhaps it's just a fish or a little duck.'

As she swam closer, she saw a mouse. He was swimming in the pool of tears, like Alice.

'Perhaps the mouse will help me,' she thought. 'Mice can't usually speak, but perhaps this one can. Everything is so strange today. I'll try to talk to him.'

'Please, Mouse. Do you know the way out of this pool? I'm very tired,' Alice asked politely.

The Mouse looked at Alice, but he said nothing.

'Perhaps he doesn't speak English,' she thought. 'Perhaps he's a French mouse. I'll speak to him in French. Now, what shall I say?'

Alice thought of the first page of her French school book. 'I'll say, "Where's my cat?" in French,' she decided. 'I know how to say that.' She said, *'Ou est ma chatte?'*

At this, the Mouse started to shake and splash.

'Oh, I'm sorry!' said Alice. 'I forgot. Mice don't like cats.'

'We do not like cats!' cried the Mouse. His voice was high and squeaky.

'Please don't be upset!' said Alice. 'Cats aren't so bad, really. I have a pretty cat called Dinah. She sits by the fire and washes her paws and her face. And she's very good at catching mice – oh, I'm sorry!'

The Mouse was shaking and splashing again.

'I won't talk about cats anymore because it upsets you so much,' said Alice quickly. 'Do you like dogs? A very nice little dog lives near my house. He has bright eyes and long, curly, brown fur. And he's very clever. If you throw a stick, he'll run and get it. He belongs to a farmer. The farmer says that his little dog catches lots of rats and – oh, I've upset you again.'

This time, the Mouse swam away from Alice, as fast as he could go.

'Dear Mouse,' called Alice. 'Please come back. I won't talk about cats or dogs again.'

The Mouse turned and swam slowly back to her. 'You must promise,' he told Alice.

'I promise,' she said. 'I won't say anything about cats or dogs.'

'Thank you,' said the Mouse. 'And now it's time to leave the pool of tears. Come with me. Let's all go together. When we get to the shore, I'll tell you my story. You'll find out why I don't like cats and dogs.'

Alice looked around her. The pool was now full of animals and birds. She saw a white duck and a dodo, a green parrot and an eagle, an orange crab with her daughter and lots more. They all swam to the shore and climbed out of the pool of tears.

CHAPTER 3

A very strange race

Alice, the Mouse and all the other animals and birds sat in a circle. They were sad because they were cold and wet after their long swim.

'How can we get dry?' they asked each other. They all started to think of ideas.

'Sit down and listen to me!' cried the Mouse after a while. 'I'll give you a long history lesson. By the time I've finished, we'll be dry.'

'I hope he's right,' thought Alice. She was very cold and wet, and she did not want to be ill.

But the Parrot said, 'We don't need a history lesson, thank you.'

'Did you speak?' asked the Mouse in an important voice.

'No!' said the Parrot quickly.

All the animals and birds sat down and looked at the Mouse.

'Are you all ready?' the Mouse said. Then he started his history lesson, but the other animals did not listen.

After a few minutes, he asked Alice, 'How are you now, my dear?'

'I'm still cold and wet,' Alice replied sadly.

The Dodo, who was a large, important-looking bird, stood up. 'I know a good way to get dry,' he said. 'We can have a race!'

'A race?' asked Alice. 'What sort of race?'

'I'll show you,' replied the Dodo. 'First we need a race track.' He drew a large circle on the ground. 'It can be any shape,' he said. 'But a circle is as good as anything.'

Then the Dodo said, 'We're ready now. Let's start the race!

'But you haven't told us the rules yet!' cried Alice. 'All races have rules. Where's the start? Where's the finish?'

'Oh, there are no rules,' said the Dodo. 'Now, stand on the track. Anywhere you like. Go!'

And so the race began. Some of the animals and birds started to run round the circle, but others waited for a few minutes. When they wanted to, they stopped running.

'This is a very strange race. How will we know when it's over?' wondered Alice. 'And how will we know who's the winner?'

The race continued. After about half an hour, the animals and birds were all dry again.

'The race is over!' the Dodo called out.

All the animals and birds crowded round the Dodo. 'Who won the race?' they asked excitedly. 'Tell us who won!'

The Dodo did not answer. He stood very still with his beak in his hand and they all waited silently. Then he cried, 'Everyone has won! Everyone gets a prize!'

They all thought about this.

'Who will give the prizes?' asked the Duck.

The Dodo pointed his finger at Alice. 'She'll do it,' he said.

Everyone crowded round Alice, calling out, 'Prizes! Prizes! Give us our prizes!'

'What should I do?' thought Alice. 'I don't have any prizes.' She put her hand into her pocket. 'I hope there's something in here,' she thought.

Luckily, she found a little box of sweets. They were still dry and there were enough for everyone. She gave a sweet to each animal and bird.

Then the Mouse pointed to Alice and said, 'She must have a prize, too.'

'You're quite right,' replied the Dodo. He turned to Alice. 'Is there anything else in your pocket?' he asked.

Alice put her hand in her pocket again. 'There's only a button,' she replied sadly. 'A button isn't a very good prize.'

But the Dodo said, 'Give it to me.'

Everyone crowded round Alice again as the Dodo gave her the button. Then they all cheered.

Alice wanted to laugh because the prizes, like the race, were very silly. But she did not. She thanked the Dodo politely.

Then the animals and birds ate their sweets. When they finished, they asked the Mouse to tell them a story.

'You can tell your story about why you hate cats and dogs so much,' said Alice to the Mouse. 'You promised to tell me.'

The Mouse turned to Alice and sighed. 'My tale is very long and very sad,' he said.

Alice looked at his tail. 'It *is* very long,' she agreed. 'But why is it sad? I don't understand.'

The Mouse did not reply. He started to tell his tale. Alice was not listening properly because she was still thinking about his tail.

The Mouse stopped speaking and turned to her. 'You're not listening to me,' he said angrily. 'What are you thinking about?'

'I'm sorry,' said Alice. 'I'm thinking about your tail. You must tell us why it's sad.'

'I will not,' cried the Mouse.

'Did you say "knot"?' asked Alice. 'Where is it? Is it in your tail? I'll untie it for you.' (She was a helpful child and could tie her own shoelaces.)

But the Mouse was very angry now. 'You're talking nonsense!' he cried. 'I won't listen to any more.' He stood up and walked away.

'Please come back, Mouse,' said Alice. 'I'm sorry if I upset you. Come back and finish your story.'

'Yes, come back!' said all the other animals and birds.

But the Mouse shook his head and ran off. The animals and birds sighed.

Alice thought about her cat. 'I wish Dinah was here,' she said. 'She could bring the Mouse back.'

'Who's Dinah?' asked the Parrot.

'Oh, she's my dear cat!' cried Alice. 'She's very good at catching mice. She catches birds, too – and then she eats them!'

The birds were not very happy about this. They quickly started to leave.

The Eagle said, 'I must go home now – this cold air makes me ill.'

'Come on, my dears,' the Duck called to her ducklings. 'It's time for bed.'

The animals went too and soon Alice was all alone.

'The trouble started when I told them about Dinah,' Alice said to herself. 'My new friends don't like her. But she's the best cat in the world! I don't understand. Oh, my dear Dinah. Will I ever see you again?' Alice started to cry because she felt so sad and lonely.

Then she heard little footsteps and she quickly dried her eyes. She was smiling now. 'The Mouse is coming back,' she thought. 'He's not angry now and he's coming back to finish his story.'

CHAPTER 4

A lizard called Bill

The Mouse did not come back. It was the White Rabbit again. 'The Duchess won't like this,' he cried, looking round. 'Oh, my paws and whiskers! Where did I drop ıem?'

'He's lost his gloves and his fan again,' thought Alice. he started to look for them. She did not know where they /ere because the long room, the little glass table and the ool of tears had all disappeared.

When the White Rabbit saw Alice, he shouted angrily, Mary Ann! What are you doing here? Go home and get ıe a pair of gloves and a fan! Be quick!'

'He thinks I'm his servant,' thought Alice. 'But I'll help im and get him some gloves and a fan.' And she ran own the path.

Soon she came to a little house, with 'W. Rabbit' on the oor. She went in and climbed the stairs. There was a little oom with a table by the window. On the table, she found hree pairs of white gloves and a fan, and she picked them p. Then she saw a bottle.

'There's no label, but I'll drink it,' she thought. 'I know omething interesting will happen.' So she picked up the ottle and drank.

'I'm growing bigger again!' she realized after a moment. She grew and grew. Soon she had to sit on the floor. Then she had to lie down. Before long, she could not fit into the room, so she put her foot up the chimney. Then she put her arm out of the window. Luckily, then she stopped growing.

'This place is so strange,' she thought. 'Everything is like a story. I'll write a book about it when I grow up. Oh, but I'm grown up *now*!' She started to laugh.

Then Alice heard a voice.

'Mary Ann! Get me my gloves and my fan!' the voice said. It was the White Rabbit. He ran up the stairs.

'I'm not afraid of him!' said Alice to herself. 'I'm much bigger than he is now!'

The White Rabbit tried to open the door, but Alice's arm was pressed against it.

'The door won't open,' said the White Rabbit, 'so I'll climb through the window.'

'No, you won't,' thought Alice. When she heard him outside the window, she tried to grab him with her hand. She did not catch him, but she heard a loud crash and a squeak.

'He's fallen on some glass,' thought Alice.

Then she heard the White Rabbit again. 'Pat! Where are you?' he said angrily.

'I'm digging for apples, sir,' said Pat.

'Pat must be another servant,' thought Alice.

'Digging for apples?' said the White Rabbit. 'What nonsense! Now, Pat, come and help me. Something is sticking out of the window. What is it?'

'It's an arm, sir,' Pat replied.

'But it's huge! Take it away, Pat,' said the White Rabbit.

There was a long silence. Alice tried to grab the White Rabbit again. This time, she heard a loud crash and two squeaks. She heard Pat and the White Rabbit whispering.

'What are they going to do?' Alice wondered. 'Perhaps they're going to pull me through the window. Well, I hope they do!'

For a while, there was silence. Alice waited. Then she heard the sound of wheels and people talking. 'They're bringing a cart,' she thought.

Then she heard the White Rabbit say, 'Where's the other ladder? ... Oh, Bill's got it. Bring it here, Bill. ... Tie the ladders together and put them here. ... Now, who's going to climb onto the roof and down the chimney?'

Lots of voices replied to this:

'Not me!'

'Not me!'

'Not me!'

'Bill will do it,' said the White Rabbit.

'Poor Bill,' thought Alice. 'He's coming down the chimney, is he?'

When she heard a sound in the chimney above her, she pulled her leg back and kicked as hard as she could.

'Look at Bill!' a voice said. 'He's flying through the air! Catch him, someone!'

And then another voice, 'That's right. Hold his head up. What happened, Bill?'

'I don't know,' said Bill. 'I went down the chimney, and then something kicked me and I was up in the air!'

'I wonder what they'll do next,' thought Alice. 'Perhaps they'll take the roof off.'

Then she heard the White Rabbit's voice. 'I've got an idea!' he said. 'Let's light a fire and burn the house down!'

'You will not,' shouted Alice. 'If you do, I'll tell my cat Dinah to chase you all! And she'll catch you!'

There was silence. Then she heard the White Rabbit saying, 'Come on, everyone. Throw them all through the window.'

Lots of little stones came through the window. Some of them hit Alice's face. 'Don't do that again!' she cried.

Then she saw that the stones were turning into little cakes. 'I'll eat one,' Alice said to herself. 'Something will happen to me, I'm sure. I can't get any bigger, so perhaps I'll get smaller.'

So Alice ate one of the little cakes. 'I was right!' she thought. 'I'm shrinking!'

As soon as she was small enough, she ran down the stairs and out of the door.

Lots of animals and birds were waiting outside the little house. Alice saw Bill the Lizard, who was sitting on the ground drinking water from a bottle. When the animals and birds saw Alice, they all ran towards her, but she ran away as fast as she could.

Soon, Alice was standing in a dark forest. 'I'm safe now,' she thought. 'First I need to grow to the right size, then I can look for the beautiful garden.'

Suddenly, she heard a barking sound, coming from somewhere above her head. She looked up and saw a huge puppy. (Of course, the puppy was not really huge. But Alice thought he was because she was so small.)

The puppy tried to touch Alice with his paw. He had large, round eyes and a short, curly tail.

'I hope he's friendly,' Alice thought. 'If he wanted to, he could eat me because he's so big! But he looks friendly, so I'll play with him.'

She picked up a stick and threw it. The puppy jumped up, grabbed the stick and brought it back to Alice. She threw the stick again.

They played with the stick until the puppy was tired. He gave a happy little bark, then he lay on the ground and closed his eyes.

'He's going to sleep. Now I can escape,' thought Alice and she started to run.

'I'll stop and rest now,' thought Alice. She sat down under a flower.

'He was a nice puppy,' she thought. 'I would like to teach him some tricks – but I'm much too small. I must find something to eat or drink and perhaps I'll grow.' Alice looked around her. She saw flowers and grass, but nothing to eat or drink. She went further into the forest.

Alice found a mushroom under a tree. 'The mushroom is taller than I am,' she thought. She looked under it and behind it. Then she looked over the edge. A large blue caterpillar was sitting on top of the mushroom.

CHAPTER 5

Alice and the Caterpillar

Alice looked at the Caterpillar and the Caterpillar looked at Alice. After a few minutes, the Caterpillar asked, 'Who are you?'

'I – I don't really know,' replied Alice slowly. 'This morning I was Alice, but so many strange things have happened. I shrank and then I grew and then I shrank again. It's very confusing.'

'No, it isn't,' said the Caterpillar.

'Oh, yes, it is. One day, you'll turn into a butterfly,' said Alice. 'You'll think that's very confusing.'

'No, I won't,' said the Caterpillar. 'And you still haven't told me who you are.'

Alice was angry with him. 'Tell me who you are first,' he said.

'Why?' replied the Caterpillar.

'If you can't be polite to me, I'm leaving,' said Alice. She started to walk away.

'Come back!' cried the Caterpillar. 'I want to tell you something.'

Alice turned and walked back to the mushroom. 'What is it?' she asked.

'You were angry with me. Never be angry!' said the Caterpillar. After a few minutes, he asked, 'How big do you want to be?'

'I want to be much bigger than this. Your mushroom is taller than I am. I'm too small now,' said Alice.

'Too small?' cried the Caterpillar. 'Too small? You're the same size as me. It's the right size.'

'But it's the wrong size for me!' said poor Alice.

'You'll get used to it,' said the Caterpillar in a sleepy voice. After a few minutes, the Caterpillar yawned. He crawled slowly down from the mushroom and along the ground. As he went, he said, 'One side will make you bigger and the other side will make you smaller.'

Alice was confused. What did he mean? 'One side of what?' she asked.

The Caterpillar replied, 'One side of the mushroom, of course!' Then he crawled away into the long grass.

Alice looked at the mushroom. 'It's a circle,' she said to herself. 'So how can it have two sides?'

She thought about this for a few minutes. Then she stretched her arms round the mushroom and broke off one piece with each hand. She looked at the two pieces of mushroom.

'Which piece will make me bigger and which piece will make me smaller?' she wondered. 'I'll eat some and find out.'

She ate some of the mushroom in her right hand.

Alice shrank so much and so fast that her chin touched her feet. 'I'm much too small now,' she thought. 'I'll try the other piece of mushroom. I hope it will make me grow bigger.' So she ate some of the mushroom in her left hand.

This time, her neck grew much longer and soon her head was a long way from her feet. She looked down. She couldn't see her shoulders, but she could see a very long neck and hundreds of green leaves.

'Why are all these leaves here?' wondered Alice. She looked down again. 'It's the tops of the trees!' she said. 'I'm taller than the trees.'

And then something flew into Alice's face. It was a large bird. She started to hit Alice with her wings, screaming, 'Snake! Snake!'

'I'm not a snake!' said Alice. 'Stop hitting me and go away!'

The Bird started to cry. 'Snakes! They always find them,' the Bird said.

'What does the Bird mean?' Alice wondered. She waited to hear more.

'They always find my eggs,' the Bird said. 'If I put them in the roots of a tree or in the grass, the snakes always find them. I can't sleep at night because I'm waiting for the snakes. They want to eat my eggs, you see.'

Now Alice understood. 'I'm so sorry,' she said. 'That must be terrible for you.'

'Today, I flew to the top of the tallest tree in the forest,' the Bird said. '"The snakes won't come up here," I thought. So I made a nest and laid some eggs in it. And then, a huge snake came down from the sky! Snake!'

'I'm not a snake,' cried Alice. 'I'm a …'

'What are you?' asked the Bird. 'Tell me the truth.'

'I'm a little girl,' said Alice slowly. But was she? She looked down at her long neck. She was not very little now!

'Nonsense!' said the Bird. 'I've seen lots of little girls. Little girls don't have long necks like that! No, you're a snake and that's the truth. Snakes like to eat eggs. Do you like to eat eggs?'

'Yes, I do,' replied Alice. (She was a very truthful child.) 'Lots of little girls eat eggs.'

'Well, if they do, they must be snakes. That's all I can say,' said the Bird.

What a strange idea! Alice was silent for a few minutes, thinking about it.

Then the Bird said, 'You're looking for eggs. I know you are. You may be a little girl or you may be a snake. It's all the same to me.'

'It's not all the same to me!' cried Alice. 'Snakes are very different from little girls. But I'm not looking for eggs, I promise.'

'Off you go, then,' said the Bird. She went back to her nest.

Alice bent down among the trees. Her long neck got stuck in the branches, but after a few minutes, her neck was free.

She still had the two pieces of mushroom in her hands. 'One piece will make me bigger and one piece will make me smaller,' she thought. 'So if I eat some of each piece, I'll soon be the right size.'

So she ate some from one piece and some from the other and so on, until she was the right size again.

'This feels very strange,' thought Alice as she walked through the forest. 'I've been so many different sizes today that it feels strange to be the right size. Perhaps I can find the beautiful garden now.'

She came to a gap in the trees and in front of her she saw a tiny house.

'I wonder who lives there?' she said to herself. 'But I can't knock on the door because I'm too big. I don't want to frighten anyone.'

So she ate some more of the piece of mushroom in her right hand. Then she put it into her right pocket. She put the piece in her left hand into her left pocket. When she was small enough, she walked up to the house.

CHAPTER 6

A baby and the Cheshire Cat

Alice looked at the tiny house. 'What shall I do now?' she wondered.

Then someone ran out of the forest and knocked on the door.

'He must be a servant,' thought Alice, 'because he's wearing a uniform. But he looks like a fish!'

Another servant opened the door. This one looked like a frog, but he was wearing a uniform, too. Alice went closer to hear what they were saying.

The Fish held out a very large letter. 'This is for the Duchess, from the Queen of Hearts,' he said in an important voice. 'It's an invitation to play croquet.'

'From the Queen of Hearts. An invitation for the Duchess. To play croquet,' replied the Frog.

Alice knew what croquet was. It was a game in which the players hit balls through metal hoops using long sticks.

The two servants bowed to each other and accidentally banged their heads together. 'Ow!' cried the servants, rubbing their heads.

Alice started to laugh. 'I don't want the servants to hear me laughing at them,' she thought. She ran back a little way into the forest. When she came back, the door was closed and the Fish was sitting on the grass.

Alice walked up to the house and knocked on the door.

'They won't hear you,' said the Fish. 'They're making too much noise.'

This was true. Alice could hear screaming and sneezing inside the house, and sometimes a loud crash. 'So how can I get in?' she asked. (Alice was a very polite child.)

'You can't,' the Fish replied.

'That's not very helpful,' thought Alice.

Then the door opened and a large plate flew out. It hit the Fish's nose.

'How can I get in?' Alice asked again.

'You can't,' replied the Fish.

'Then what shall I do?' said Alice.

'Anything you like,' said the Fish. He started to whistle.

Alice sighed. 'I'll just go in,' she said and she opened the door.

Alice went into a large kitchen, which was full of smoke. In the middle of the room, the Duchess was sitting on a stool with three legs. She was holding a red-faced baby, who was screaming. A cook was stirring a pot of soup over a fire.

Alice started to sneeze. 'Achoo!' she cried. 'The cook has put too much pepper in that soup.'

The Duchess and the baby started to sneeze, too. But the cook did not sneeze and neither did the large striped cat who sat by the fire. The cat had a huge smile on his face.

'Why is your cat smiling?' Alice asked the Duchess.

'Because he's a Cheshire Cat!' the Duchess replied.

Alice was confused. '*Can* a cat smile?' she said.

'Oh, yes,' said the Duchess. 'All cats can smile and most of them do.'

'I don't know any cats who can smile,' said Alice.

'Then you don't know much,' said the Duchess. 'And that's a fact.'

The cook lifted the pot of soup from the fire. Then she
started to throw things at the Duchess. First she threw the
soup spoon, and then pots and pans, plates, dishes, cups,
knives and forks … Then a large pot flew through the air
towards the baby.

'Please, stop that!' cried Alice, jumping up and down.
You'll hit his poor little nose!'

'Be quiet!' shouted the Duchess. She started to rock the
baby in her arms, singing to it all the time. At the end of
each line of the song, she threw the baby high into the air.
He screamed so loudly that Alice could not hear the words.
Then the Duchess pushed the baby into Alice's arms.

'You can look after him now,' the Duchess said. 'I must get ready for the croquet game.' And off she went.

As the Duchess left the kitchen, the cook threw a large pan at her back. It landed on the floor with a crash.

The baby was crying and wriggling, sticking out his arms and legs.

'He looks like a starfish,' thought Alice. 'Poor little thing! But I don't know how to look after a baby. I'll leave him here.' She laid the baby gently down on a chair and left the house.

As Alice walked through the forest, she thought someone was watching her. She looked up and saw the Cheshire Cat sitting in a tree.

He smiled at Alice.

'He looks friendly,' thought Alice. 'But he has very long claws and sharp teeth. I'll speak to him very politely.'

'Please, Cheshire Cat, can you tell me which way I should walk?' she began.

'Well, where do you want to go?' he replied.

'I – I don't know,' said Alice.

'Then it doesn't matter which way you walk,' said the Cheshire Cat with a big smile.

'That's true,' thought Alice. 'I'll ask him something else. She said, 'Who lives in this forest?'

The Cheshire Cat waved his right paw in the air and said, 'If you go that way, you'll come to the Mad Hatter's house.' He waved his left paw. 'If you go that way, you'll

come to the March Hare's house. They're both mad. We're all mad here – I'm mad and you're mad.'

'I'm not mad!' cried Alice.

'You must be mad, if you're here,' the Cheshire Cat replied.

Alice didn't agree with that. But she said, 'How do you know you're mad?'

'Well,' he said. 'A dog isn't mad, is he? A dog growls when he's angry and wags his tail when he's happy. I growl when I'm happy and wag my tail when I'm angry. So I must be mad.'

'A cat doesn't growl,' said Alice. 'A cat purrs.'

'Call it what you like,' said the Cheshire Cat. 'Are you going to play croquet with the Queen today?' he asked, suddenly.

'I hope I am,' said Alice. 'But she hasn't invited me yet.'

'If you go, I'll see you there,' said the Cheshire Cat. And he started to disappear very slowly. First his tail

disappeared, then his legs, then his body and then his head. Last of all, his smile slowly disappeared.

'That's very strange,' Alice thought. 'I've seen a cat without a smile. But I've never seen a smile without a cat!'

'Now I'll try to find the March Hare's house,' thought Alice. She started walking along the path on the left.

'I've seen hatters before,' Alice said. 'They make hats. But I've never seen a March Hare. He'll be much more interesting, I think. Anyway, it's May now, not March, so perhaps he won't still be mad.'

She went on through the forest and soon she came to a large house. 'I think the March Hare lives here,' she thought. 'The chimneys look like long pointed ears and there's fur on the roof! But I can't open the gate. I must grow bigger before I can go in.'

She ate some of the piece of mushroom from her left pocket and soon she was big enough to open the gate.

CHAPTER 7

The tea party

Outside the house, Alice saw a table under a tree. The March Hare and the Mad Hatter were sitting at it, drinking tea. A fat Dormouse sat between them with his eyes closed. He looked sleepy.

The table was very large, with teacups and saucers set out all around it. But when the March Hare and the Mad Hatter saw Alice, they cried, 'There's no room! No room!'

Alice was confused. 'But there's lots of room!' she replied. She sat down at the end of the table.

'Would you like some cake?' asked the March Hare.

Alice looked round the table. 'I can't see any cake,' she replied.

'There isn't any!' said the March Hare.

'Why did you ask me if I wanted some, then?' asked Alice.

'Why did you come to a tea party when you weren't invited?' answered the March Hare angrily.

The Mad Hatter spoke for the first time. 'Your hair is too long,' he said to Alice.

'And you're very rude,' she replied.

Next came a riddle. 'Why is a raven like a writing desk?' asked the Mad Hatter.

'Oh, good! I like riddles,' said Alice. 'I'll try to guess the answer.'

But then the Mad Hatter took his watch from his pocket and shook it. 'It's broken,' he said angrily to the March Hare. 'Did you put butter on it?'

'Yes, I did. But it was the *best* butter,' replied the March Hare sadly.

'Did you put it on with the bread knife?' asked the Mad Hatter. 'There are some breadcrumbs in it, too.'

The March Hare looked sadly at the watch and put it in his tea. He looked at it again. 'It was the very best butter,' he said, shaking his head sadly.

Then the Mad Hatter said, 'The Dormouse is asleep again.' He put some jam on the Dormouse's nose. 'That will wake him up!' he said.

He turned to Alice. 'Have you guessed the riddle yet?' he asked.

'No,' she sighed. 'Tell me the answer.'

'There *is* no answer!' replied the Mad Hatter.

Alice sighed again. 'You're wasting time,' she said, 'asking riddles that have no answers.'

'Long ago,' said the Mad Hatter, 'Time was my friend. When I asked him to, he changed the time for me. One day, when it was nine o'clock in the morning, Time changed it to half-past one. Time for lunch!'

'Time for lunch!' whispered the March Hare.

'But were you hungry when it was really only nine o'clock?' Alice asked the Mad Hatter.

'No, but it was half-past one for a long time,' he replied. 'Anyway, Time and I had an argument. It was in March, just before the March Hare went mad.' The Mad Hatter pointed his teaspoon at the March Hare. 'We were at the Queen of Hearts' party and I had to sing a song,' he said. 'It went like this:

Twinkle, twinkle, little bat,
How I wonder what you're at.
Up above the world you fly,
Like a tea tray in the sky,
Twinkle, twinkle, little bat,
How I wonder what you're at!'

The Dormouse woke up and started to sing, 'Twinkle, twinkle, twinkle …'

The Mad Hatter pushed him to make him stop. 'Do you

know that song?' he asked Alice.

'I think I do,' she replied.

'After the first verse, the Queen shouted, "He's killing the time!" She meant that I was singing to the wrong rhythm. But after that, Time was my enemy! He thought I was trying to kill him. He won't do as I ask him and it's always six o'clock here! Always tea time,' said the Mad Hatter.

'So that's why you need lots of cups and saucers!' Alice said.

'Yes,' said the Mad Hatter. 'When we've finished our tea, we move round the table and start again.'

'What happens when you reach the beginning of the table again?' wondered Alice.

The March Hare yawned. 'I'm bored,' he said to Alice. 'Will you tell us a story?'

'I'm sorry, but I don't know any stories,' said Alice quickly.

'Then the Dormouse will tell one. Wake up!' the March Hare said.

He pushed the Dormouse, who slowly opened his eyes. 'Tell us a story before you go to sleep again!' said the March Hare.

'Once upon a time,' the Dormouse began, 'there were three little sisters. Their names were Elsie, Lacie and Tillie, and they lived at the bottom of a well ...'

'What did they eat?' asked Alice.

'Jam,' said the Dormouse.

'That can't be right!' replied Alice. 'If you only ate jam, you would be very ill.'

'They *were* very ill,' the Dormouse told her.

Then the Mad Hatter said to Alice, 'Would you like some more tea?'

'I haven't had any yet, so I can't have more,' said Alice, pouring some tea into a cup. Then she asked the Dormouse, 'Why did they live at the bottom of a well?'

'It was a jam well,' said the Dormouse.

'I've never seen a jam well!' said Alice. 'You made that up!'

'If you're going to be rude,' said the Dormouse, 'you can finish the story yourself.'

'I'm sorry,' said Alice. 'Please continue.'

'The three little sisters were learning to draw,' the Dormouse said.

'What did they draw?' asked Alice.

'They drew jam,' he replied.

Then the Mad Hatter said, 'I want a clean cup. Let's all move round the table.'

He moved to the place on his left, the Dormouse moved to the Mad Hatter's place, the March Hare moved to the Dormouse's place and Alice moved to the March Hare's place.

Of course, the only one who had a clean cup was the Mad Hatter. And poor Alice now had a saucer full of milk that the March Hare had spilt.

The Dormouse sleepily continued with his story. 'They were learning to draw other things, too. Not just jam. Things whose names begin with "M".'

'Why "M"?' asked Alice.

'Why not?' replied the Dormouse, closing his eyes. The Mad Hatter pushed him to wake him up again.

'Ouch!' said the Dormouse. 'They drew a mouse, the moon, madness and much ...'

'I don't think ...' Alice began.

'Then don't talk!' said the Mad Hatter.

Alice thought this was so rude that she stood up and walked away.

When she looked back, the Mad Hatter and the March Hare were trying to put the Dormouse in the teapot.

'I won't go back there,' said Alice to herself as she walked through the forest. 'What a strange tea party!'

There was a big tree on her left and she saw that there was a door in it. 'I think I'll go through that door,' she said. 'I'm sure something strange will happen.' So she opened the door and went through it.

Alice was now in the long room again and she could see the glass table with the tiny gold key on it. She picked up the key and unlocked the little door to the beautiful garden.

'I'm too big to go in,' she thought. 'But I still have a piece of the mushroom in my right pocket.' She started to nibble it and soon she was small enough to go through the door. At last, she was in the beautiful garden, among the pink and white flowers, the fruit trees and the cool water fountains.

CHAPTER 8

A game of croquet

The first thing Alice saw was a tall rose tree covered in beautiful white roses. But something strange was happening to it. Three gardeners were holding pots of paint and they were painting the roses red! And all the gardeners were cards – the two, five and seven of Spades.

Alice decided to watch and she went closer.

'Stop that, Five!' said Two. 'You're splashing paint on me!'

'Be angry with Seven, not me. He pushed me!' replied Five.

Seven looked up from his work and said, 'That's right, Five. Always blame someone else for your mistakes!'

'Be quiet, Seven,' said Five. 'The Queen was talking about you yesterday. She said you're going to prison!'

'Why?' asked Two.

'I'm not going to tell you,' said Seven.

'Well, I'll tell him,' cried Five. 'The cook told him to dig up some onions from the garden. But he didn't dig up onions, he dug up flower bulbs!'

Seven angrily threw his paintbrush on the ground. Then the gardeners saw Alice and they all bowed to her.

'Will you tell me, please, why you're painting those roses?' Alice asked.

Five and Seven looked at Two, who looked at his feet. Then he said, 'We made a mistake, miss. The Queen wanted a red rose tree, but we planted a white one. If she finds out, she'll send us to prison! So we're painting the roses red.'

Five was looking across the garden. Suddenly, he cried out, 'It's the Queen! The Queen is coming!'

All the gardeners threw themselves down, with their faces touching the ground. Alice could hear the footsteps of soldiers marching and she waited with the gardeners to see the Queen.

Ten soldiers came first, marching in pairs. Like the gardeners, they were all cards – Clubs this time. Ten servants came next – they were all Diamonds. The children of the King and Queen of Hearts came after the servants, skipping along happily. The children were cards, too – Hearts, of course.

The Queen's guests followed the royal children. Most of the guests were kings and queens, but Alice saw the White

Rabbit with them. He was talking and smiling, and he did not see Alice.

The Jack of Hearts came after the guests. He was carrying the King's crown on a red velvet cushion. Last of all were the King and Queen of Hearts!

'Shall I throw myself on the ground, like the gardeners?' wondered Alice. 'But that's silly. If everyone did that, they wouldn't see the Queen!'

The Queen stopped and looked at Alice. 'Who's this?' she asked the Jack of Hearts.

He did not know, so he just smiled.

'Fool!' shouted the Queen and turned back to Alice. 'What's your name, child?' she asked.

'My name's Alice, Your Majesty,' she replied politely. But she thought, 'They're only cards! I'm not afraid of a pack of cards!'

'And who are these?' asked the Queen, pointing her finger at the three gardeners. She could only see their backs, of course.

'I don't know,' said Alice.

At this, the Queen's face turned red. 'Send her to prison!' she cried.

'Nonsense,' Alice replied and the Queen was silent.

She turned to the Jack of Hearts. 'Turn them over,' the Queen said.

The Jack of Hearts turned the three gardeners over with his foot. The gardeners all jumped up and they started to bow.

'Stop that!' cried the Queen. 'What have you done with that red paint? Send them to prison!'

The Queen and everyone else moved on, leaving three soldiers to take the gardeners to prison.

'Don't worry,' Alice told the gardeners. 'You won't go to prison.' She hid the gardeners in a large flower pot and then she joined the Queen.

'Can you play croquet?' the Queen asked Alice as they walked along.

Alice said that she could and the Queen cried, 'Come with us! The game will start soon!'

Then the White Rabbit came up to Alice.

'Hello!' Alice said. 'The Duchess isn't here. Do you know where she is?'

'The Queen has sent her to prison!' replied the White Rabbit. 'She hit the Queen on the nose with a spoon!'

'Oh dear!' Alice said.

'The game of croquet will now begin!' cried the Queen. Go to your places!'

The players started running about and bumping into each other, but after a few minutes they were all ready. n a normal game of croquet, the players have to hit balls hrough metal hoops. They use long sticks called mallets to it the balls. Alice knew that, but this game of croquet was very different.

The ground was not flat, and there were lots of holes nd bumps. The balls were hedgehogs and the mallets vere pink flamingoes! The soldiers stood on their feet and hands and arched their backs – these were the hoops.

Alice picked up her flamingo and put it under her arm with its legs hanging down. She made its neck straight and got ready to hit her hedgehog. But the flamingo twisted its head round and looked at Alice, and so she started to laugh.

When the flamingo was ready again, the hedgehog crawled away. The 'hoops' would not stay in their places – they stood up and walked about.

Nobody waited for their turn to play and there were lots of arguments. The Queen was soon very angry, marching about and saying, 'Send them to prison!'

'All the prisons must be full,' thought Alice. 'I hope she doesn't send me to one of them.' Then she saw something above her head. It looked like a smile. It *was* a smile!

'It's the Cheshire Cat!' said Alice to herself. 'A friend, at last!'

When his mouth appeared, the Cheshire Cat said, 'Are you enjoying the game?'

Alice waited for his ears to appear and then she replied, 'Not really. They don't play fairly. They fight all the time and there are no rules. The hoops move around, the balls crawl away …'

'And do you like the Queen?' asked the Cheshire Cat, as the rest of his head appeared.

'No, I don't,' replied Alice. 'She's very ...' Then she saw that the Queen was listening. 'She's very good at croquet,' she said.

The Queen smiled proudly. Then the King spoke to Alice. 'Who are you talking to?' he asked.

'My friend, the Cheshire Cat,' she replied.

The King looked at the Cheshire Cat's head. 'I don't like him,' he said. 'But he may kiss my hand.'

'I will not!' said the Cheshire Cat.

'You're very rude!' cried the King. 'Come here, my dear and get rid of this cat!' he said to the Queen.

'I'll happily do that!' replied the Queen. 'Send him to prison!'

Alice went back to the game of croquet. Three players had been sent to prison. When she tried to find her hedgehog, it was fighting with another hedgehog. Her flamingo was trying to fly up into a tree and all the hoops had disappeared.

Then Alice heard a loud cry: 'Everyone must come to the court building! The trial is starting.'

'We're going to court!' thought Alice. 'Someone must have done something wrong!'

CHAPTER 9

Who stole the tarts?

Everyone went into the court building. Lots of animals and birds were there, and Alice could see the whole pack of cards – the Spades, the Clubs, the Hearts and the Diamonds.

The Jack of Hearts was a prisoner in chains, guarded by two soldiers. The White Rabbit stood near the Jack, holding a trumpet and a piece of paper. Alice saw a plate of jam tarts in the middle of the court and she started to feel hungry. 'I hope we can eat them later,' she thought.

'I think that's the judge,' she said to herself, looking at a man wearing a long, grey wig on his head. He was sitting on a big throne next to the Queen.

'The judge is the person in charge of the court,' Alice thought. 'But he's wearing a crown as well! Oh, it's the King of Hearts! And I can see the jury.'

Alice knew that the jury are the twelve people who

decide whether the prisoner has done something wrong. They sit in a jury box.

The members of the jury were all animals and birds. They were writing in their notebooks. One of them was Bill the Lizard, who was writing very noisily with a squeaky pencil. This made Alice angry and she took it away from him.

Suddenly, the White Rabbit cried, 'Silence in court!' Then he blew his trumpet and said:

The Queen of Hearts, she made some tarts,
Upon a summer day.
The Jack of Hearts, he stole those tarts,
And took them all away!

'Call the first witness!' said the King.

Alice knew that a witness is a person who has seen someone doing something wrong. He goes to court to talk about what he saw.

The first witness was the Mad Hatter, who came in with the March Hare and the Dormouse. He had a cup of tea in one hand, and a piece of bread and butter in the other. 'I'm sorry, Your Majesty,' he said to the King. 'When I left to come to the court, I was still drinking my tea.'

'When did you start drinking your tea?' asked the King.

'I think it was the fourteenth of March,' replied the Mad Hatter.

'No, it was the fifteenth,' said the March Hare.

'The sixteenth,' said the Dormouse.

'Write that down,' said the King to the members of the jury. Then he said to the Mad Hatter, 'Take off your hat.'

'It isn't *my* hat,' said the Mad Hatter.

'It's stolen!' cried the King and the jury wrote it down.

'No, it isn't stolen,' said the Mad Hatter. 'It isn't my hat because I'm going to sell it. I'm a Hatter, Your Majesty. I make hats. That's my job.'

The Queen put on her glasses and stared at the Mad Hatter, who started to shake with fear. He bit off a piece of his teacup by mistake.

Then the Queen said, 'Bring me the list of singers at my last party!'

At this, the Mad Hatter shook so much that his shoes fell off.

'You're an important witness. Tell the court about the tarts!' ordered the King.

'Well, I was drinking my tea and the March Hare said …' began the Mad Hatter.

'No, I didn't,' said the March Hare.

'You did!' said the Mad Hatter.

'I didn't!' said the March Hare.

'Well, the Dormouse said …' said the Mad Hatter.

The Dormouse did not reply to this because he was aslee

'And after that,' continued the Mad Hatter, 'I made som more bread and butter …'

'But what did the Dormouse say?' asked a member of th jury.

'I can't remember,' said the poor Mad Hatter.

'You must remember,' said the King angrily, 'or I'll send you to prison.'

The Mad Hatter dropped his teacup and knelt down before the King.

'Your Majesty, I'm a good man …' he said.

'Well, you're a very bad witness,' the King told him. 'You may go.'

The Mad Hatter ran out of the court in his socks, leaving his shoes behind.

'Send him to prison!' cried the Queen, but the Mad Hatter had gone.

Two of the animals started to cheer, and the soldiers put them in a large bag and tied it up.

'Stop squashing me!' squeaked the Dormouse, who was sitting next to Alice. 'I can't breathe.'

'I'm sorry,' Alice replied. 'I think I'm growing again.' She did feel very strange.

'You can't grow here!' said the Dormouse angrily.

'You're growing, too,' Alice told him.

'Yes, but I'm growing slowly,' said the Dormouse, and he stood up and walked away.

'Call the next witness!' said the King.

The next witness was the Duchess's cook. She was carrying her pepper pot, and some of the animals and birds started to sneeze.

The King folded his arms and looked at the cook. 'What are tarts made of?' he asked her.

'Pepper,' the cook replied.

'Jam,' said a sleepy voice at the back of the court.

This made the Queen very angry. 'Send that Dormouse to prison!' she cried. 'Cut off his whiskers!'

Everyone started shouting. At last, the Dormouse was taken out of the court.

'Call the next witness!' cried the King.

The White Rabbit looked at his list of witnesses.

'Who will it be?' wondered Alice.

The White Rabbit blew his trumpet and there was silence. Then he cried, 'The next witness is – Alice!'

CHAPTER 10

Just a pack of cards

'Here I am!' said Alice. She was now much bigger than everyone else in the court. She jumped up so fast that her skirt caught the jury box, and all the animals and birds fell out.

Alice thought about her poor pet goldfish – last week she had knocked over their bowl.

'I'm very sorry,' she said. She picked up the members of the jury and put them back in their box. 'If I don't do this quickly, they will die!' she said to herself. (She was still thinking about her goldfish.)

Then the King of Hearts spoke. 'We can't go on,' he said, 'until *all* the members of the jury are back in their places.' He looked at Alice.

Alice looked at the jury box. Bill the Lizard was upside down! 'I'm stuck!' he whispered, sadly waving his tail.

Quickly, Alice picked him up and turned him over. The other members of the jury found their pencils and their notebooks and started to write notes. Poor Bill was too upset and he sat with his mouth open, staring up at the ceiling.

'Who stole the tarts?' the King asked Alice. 'What do you know about it?'

'Nothing,' replied Alice.

'Nothing?' said the King.

'Nothing,' said Alice.

'That's a very important fact,' said the King. He turned to the members of the jury. 'Write it down,' he told them.

But then the White Rabbit jumped up. 'I think you mean *un*important, Your Majesty,' he said, looking at the King.

'Yes, yes. Unimportant, of course,' said the King.

Some of the jury wrote 'important' and some wrote 'unimportant'.

'But it really doesn't matter,' thought Alice.

The King was writing in his notebook. Suddenly, he cried, 'Silence in court!' Then he read out, 'Rule 42. All people who are more than a mile high must leave the court.'

Everyone looked at Alice.

'*I'm* not a mile high!' she said.

'Yes, you are,' replied the King.

'You're nearly two miles high,' added the Queen.

'Well, I won't leave,' said Alice. 'That's not a real rule. You just wrote it down.'

'It's the oldest rule in the book,' said the King.

'Then it should be Rule 1,' said Alice.

At this, the King shut his notebook quickly and cried, It's time for the verdict!'

Alice knew that the verdict is what the judge decides at he end of the trial.

The White Rabbit jumped up and said, 'Not yet, Your Majesty. We must read this first. It's a letter from the Jack of Hearts.'

'Read it to the court,' said the King.

The White Rabbit unfolded the piece of paper and said, t isn't a letter. It's a poem.'

Then the Jack of Hearts spoke. 'I didn't write it, Your Majesty,' he said. 'No one has signed it, so you can't prove hat I wrote it.'

'You didn't sign it,' said the King, 'because you didn't rant to be caught! An honest man always signs his name.'

Everyone clapped their hands and the Queen said, 'That roves that he stole the tarts. Send him to prison!'

'It doesn't prove anything,' said Alice. 'You don't even know what the poem is about.'

'Read it!' said the King.

The White Rabbit put on his glasses and asked, 'Where shall I start, Your Majesty?'

'Start at the beginning and stop when you get to the end,' the King replied.

The White Rabbit read the poem to the court:

I gave her one, they gave him two,
You gave us three or more.
They all returned from him to you,
Though they were mine before.

'That poem is very important,' said the King, rubbing his hands together.

'No, it isn't,' said Alice. 'It's nonsense.' She was now so big that she wasn't afraid of him.

Then the King pointed his finger at the plate of tarts.

'Look!' he cried. 'Here are the tarts! Nobody stole them! Now we can have the verdict, at last.'

'No, no!' replied the Queen. 'We must have the sentence first and then the verdict.

'That's nonsense, too,' said Alice. 'The sentence is the judge's punishment for the prisoner. You can't have the sentence before the verdict!'

'Be quiet!' said the Queen. She was so angry that her face had turned purple.

'I won't be quiet!' replied Alice.

'Send her to prison!' shouted the Queen.

But nobody moved. And Alice was now the right size, so she felt very brave.

'I'm not afraid of you!' she said. 'You're just a pack of cards!'

And then the whole pack flew up into the air and crashed down on Alice's head. She screamed and tried to push the cards away …

… and then she was lying on the river bank next to her sister. Some dry leaves had fallen onto Alice's face and her sister was gently brushing them off.

'Wake up, Alice,' she said, kissing her. 'You've been asleep for a long time.'

'I had a very strange dream,' said Alice, and she told her sister about her adventures with the White Rabbit, the Mad Hatter and the others.

'It *was* a very strange dream,' her sister said when she had finished. 'But it's time for tea now. Let's go home.'

So Alice ran home for her tea, still thinking about all her exciting adventures in Wonderland.

The End

Look back at Alice's poem on page 11 and the Mad Hatter's song on page 44. Here they are with the right words!

How does the little busy bee

How does the little busy bee
Improve each shining hour,
And gather honey all the day
From every opening flower!

How skilfully she builds her cell!
How neat she spreads the wax!
And works hard to store it well
With the sweet food she makes.

Isaac Watts

Twinkle, twinkle, little star

Twinkle, twinkle, little star,
How I wonder what you are!
Up above the world so high,
Like a diamond in the sky,
Twinkle, twinkle, little star,
How I wonder what you are!

Jane Taylor

Victorian toys and games

Lewis Carroll wrote *Alice's Adventures in Wonderland* in 1865, when Queen Victoria was the queen of Great Britain. Victorian children like Alice had no televisions or computer games. They played with toys and games like these.

OUTDOOR TOYS

Children often played with balls and skipping ropes outside. Children still enjoy ball games and skipping today.

Victorian children also liked playing with hoops. They had races, rolling the metal hoops along with long sticks.

INDOOR TOYS

The first public train service started in England in 1825. Model train sets like this one were popular in Victorian times.

Children loved riding on rocking horses like this one. The horses were made of painted wood, and they had manes and tails made of hair from real horses. There were lots more real horses in Victorian England because there were no cars.

INDOOR GAMES

Board games such as *Snakes and Ladders* were very popular. Players rolled a dice and pushed their counters around the board, going down the snakes and up the ladders.

Card games were first played in China in the 7th to 10th centuries, after the invention of paper. They were brought to Europe in the late 14th century.

The cards in *Alice's Adventures in Wonderland* are the British pack. The fifty-two cards are divided into suits (sets). Each suit has a different symbol.

The four suits are Hearts, Diamonds, Spades and Clubs. Hearts and Diamonds are red, Spades and Clubs are black. Each suit has a king, a queen and a jack, as well as an ace (number 1) and the numbers 2–10.

About the author – Lewis Carroll

Lewis Carroll's real name was Charles Lutwidge Dodgson. He was born in Cheshire, England, in 1832, and he was the oldest boy in a family of eleven children. As a child, he enjoyed making up games and he was very good at maths. When he was twenty years old, he went to study maths at Oxford University and he later became a lecturer.

He knew a little girl called Alice Liddell and often told stories to her and her sisters. One day they all went on a picnic and he told them the story that became *Alice's Adventures in Wonderland*. When they arrived home, Alice asked him to write the story down and he did. It was published by Macmillan in 1865. He later wrote a second book about Alice called *Through the Looking Glass, and What Alice Found There*. There is also a Macmillan English Explorers version of this book.

Lewis Carroll was also a very good photographer. He took pictures of famous people such as the poet Alfred Lord Tennyson, as well as the children he knew.

When he died in 1898, *Alice's Adventures in Wonderland* was the most popular children's book in England. This version of the story contains the original artwork from 1865.